Ups and downs

Hachette UK's policy is to use papers that are natural, renewable and recyclable products and made from wood grown in well-managed forests and other controlled sources. The logging and manufacturing processes are expected to conform to the environmental regulations of the country of origin.

Orders: please contact Bookpoint Ltd, 130 Park Drive, Milton Park, Abingdon, Oxon OX14 4SE. Telephone: +44 (0)1235 827827. Fax: +44 (0)1235 400401.
Email education@bookpoint.co.uk
Lines are open from 9 a.m. to 5 p.m., Monday to Saturday, with a 24-hour message answering service.

You can also order through our website: www.hoddereducation.com

ISBN: 9781510481695

© Quirky Kid 2020

First published in 2016 as The Best of Friends ™ © Quirky Kid

Concept by Dr Kimberley O'Brien

Illustrations by Connah Brecon © Quirky Kid 2020

Story by Barbara Gonzalez © Quirky Kid 2020

Art direction by Leonardo Rocker

Graphic design by Lisa Diebold

This edition designed and typeset by Gary Kilpatrick

Printed in India

This edition published in 2020 by
Hodder Education,
An Hachette UK Company
Carmelite House
50 Victoria Embankment
London EC4Y 0DZ
www.hoddereducation.com

Impression number   10 9 8 7 6 5 4 3 2 1

Year   2024 2023 2022 2021 2020

A catalogue record for this title is available from the British Library.

MIX
Paper from responsible sources
FSC™ C104740
www.fsc.org

Ups and downs

Activities by
Dr Kimberley O'Brien

Story by
Barbara Gonzalez

Illustrated by
Connah Brecon

Welcome to PYP Friends!

Meet the four friends who live on Quirky Lane and follow the stories of how they resolve conflict and strengthen their friendships in the school playground and local neighbourhood.

Salma

Coco

Lochie

Rafi

It was Saturday and, as usual, Coco and Salma were upside down at the park.

Upside down?

Yes, on the monkey bars of course!

The girls swung and giggled their way across like two cheeky chimps in the jungle.

It sounded a bit like this:

"Wheeee OO OO heeeee heeeee!!"

At last they made it to the end of the bars, and with a THUD they were back on the ground.

"Ta-dah! We did it!" said Coco, triumphantly. Salma just kept giggling. "What are you laughing at?" Coco asked. "You," said Salma, "you look funny."

It was true. Coco had one pig tail on top of her head and the other behind her ear and her cheeks were bright red, like strawberries! "You look funny too!" said Coco, and she made a face to show Salma how silly she looked.

The two friends laughed even harder and their faces went even redder.

But then, suddenly, Coco looked away, into the distance. "Look over there on the big swings. It's Harriet," she said. Salma went very quiet.

Harriet was a girl from school that Salma didn't like. She never knew if Harriet was going to be kind or horrible and this bothered her a lot. Especially because Harriet had been horrible to her once before. Salma couldn't understand why Coco and all the girls at school thought she was the **'bee's knees'** and wanted to be her friend.

"I hope she comes over and plays with us," said Coco. This made Salma

even more

nervous

because she did not want Harriet to come over.

"Look Salma! I think she's coming over here!

Act natural," cried Coco.

Oh no, thought Salma to herself. At that moment, she wished with all her heart that she could make herself invisible.

"Hi Coco," said Harriet.

"Hi! I saw you playing on the swings before. It looked like fun," said Coco.

Salma felt worried. It seemed that Coco really wanted to go and play with Harriet. Even though she didn't say anything, Salma wished that her best friend would stay with her.

5

And then it happened ... before Salma could do anything, Coco was off to the play on the big swings with Harriet. She couldn't believe it. Harriet hadn't even asked her to play with them and Coco just upped and left with Harriet!

Salma felt truly invisible

and did her best to keep busy.

She played on the slide and looked for funny rocks to add to her collection. But she couldn't help looking over at Coco and Harriet laughing and playing on the big swings.

She wondered if

this meant that Coco didn't want to be her best friend any more? Her eyes stung and she felt a big lump forming in her throat.

"Salma,

are you okay?"

It was Coco's mum and, as she smiled warmly at Salma, the dogs Flip and Flop came running up to Salma and covered her in wet, doggy kisses.

Salma laughed and was

glad to have the company

of Flip and *Flop*

for a while.

She loved the way they always came back when she threw the stick for them.

Soon it was time to go home and Coco finally came back to find Salma. Coco was so excited about her new friend, Harriet, that she didn't notice that Salma wasn't very happy to see her.

As they walked home, Coco asked Salma, "Do you think Harriet will want to play with me at school on Monday?" Salma shrugged and kept her eyes down.

"Maybe," she said.

Poor Salma, she really wasn't looking forward to Monday.

11

On Monday morning at play time, Salma wasn't able to find Coco anywhere. So she walked around the playground for a while looking for her. Finally, she saw Coco playing skipping rope with Harriet and all of her friends.

Salma took a deep breath.

"It's easy, you can do this," she told herself. And then she bravely strode across the playground towards Coco, Harriet and the other girls.

"Hi," she said.

"Can I play too?"

Some of the girls said hi, but most of them ignored her. Finally Harriet said, "Actually, I don't think so. We've got enough players." Salma wished she could disappear as Harriet and her friends, and even Coco, turned around and went back to their game.

BRRRINNGG!!!

That afternoon, when the bell rang for playtime, Salma slowly made her way out to the playground. She decided to go and find Lochie and Rafi and see if she could play handball with them.

Just then, she heard someone calling her. "Hey Salma! Do you want to come and play with us?" It was Coco and she was walking with Harriet and the other girls out to the playground too.

Salma felt an **ache** in her belly, but she smiled and walked over to meet them.

She was glad Coco was inviting her to play. But just then, something unexpected happened – this time to Coco!

Cool as a cucumber, Harriet turned to Coco and said: "Actually, we've got enough players today."

Coco felt confused.

"Do you mean Salma can't play with us?" asked Coco.

"No, I mean both of you," said Harriet, and she and her friends turned and walked away, leaving Coco and Salma speechless.

Salma looked at her best friend and tried to imagine how she might be feeling.

She remembered how she had felt that day at the park and thought that perhaps Coco was feeling sad like she had felt.

"Don't worry, Coco. You've got plenty of other friends," said Salma. "That's true," said Coco. "I've got you and all the other kids on Quirky Lane too!"

Coco was **cheering up** a bit now and coming back to her usual, chatty self. "Come on, let's go and find Rafi and Lochie and play handball instead." "Great idea!" said Coco.

As they walked over to find their friends, Coco imagined how Salma might have felt those times she'd been left out.

"Salma, I'm really sorry for leaving you out,"

said Coco. "It wasn't very nice of me to do that." Salma knew that Coco would never really hurt her on purpose, but she was glad to hear the apology all the same. "That's okay." said Salma. "Don't worry about it. I'm just glad you're back."

It was true, she really was very glad to have her best friend back.

Different friends for different people

P eople bring all kinds of values and traits to their friendships. Some of these are important when it comes to building friendships, like being kind, while others help to make friendships last, like being honest. Let's find out what matters the most to you.

1 **Read and order** the characteristics below. Number **1** should be the most important to you, and number **20,** the least important. There is no wrong order.

Friendly	Cheeky	Affectionate	Smart
Bossy	Talkative	Trustworthy	Funny
Tough	Kind	Supportive	Popular
Helpful	Curious	Generous	Understanding
Polite	Honest	Inclusive	(Add your own here)

2 Now, copy your **top 10** characteristics below and add a short sentence about what each word means to **you.**

1 ....
....
....

2 ....
....
....

3 ....
....
....

4 ....
....
....

5 ....
....
....

6 ....
....
....

7 ....
....
....

8 ....
....
....

9 ....
....
....

10 ....
....
....

3 With the person next to you, **compare** how many of your top 10 characteristics **match up**, and discuss your choices and meanings.

Role play:

How to repair a broken friendship

F riendships are never perfect. A trick to make friendships last is learning how to stay calm, apologize and forgive one another when things turn sour. This is no easy task and takes practise, patience, and a great deal of empathy. Here's how it's done.

Ingredients

AWARENESS
Learn to recognize when a friendship is changing.

PLANNING
Brainstorm your own ideas to resolve the problem.

BRAVERY
Take a deep breath and trust your friend will want to resolve the problem too!

COMPROMISE
Work together to save your friendship – focus on what's working, rather than what's not.

Method

Step 1

Look for the signs to see if something is wrong.

E.g.: facial expressions, body language or what they are telling you.

Step 2

Go ahead and ask questions like, "Have I done something to upset you?" or "Is everything okay?"

Step 3

Listen carefully and try to understand how your friend is feeling. Give them lots of time to talk before you respond.

Step 4

Apologize if your friend is upset and think of something you could do or say to help the situation.

What would you say to make your friend feel better?

....

....

....

Step 5

Together, think of more ways to overcome the problem and then agree on the best way forward.

Let's practise

Read the following scenarios and answer the questions. Remember to look back at the ingredients and steps on the previous pages.

Your friend borrowed your favourite pencil sharpener and accidentally broke it. They said they would replace it, but so far ... nothing!

What signs (facial expression or body language) would tell you if your friend was sorry?

....

....

How could you resolve the problem without upsetting your friend?

....

....

Now try to role play this with your group.

Last week you peeked at your friend's spelling test and managed to get the highest mark in the class. Your friend hasn't spoken to you since.

How do you think your friend is feeling about what happened?

....

What steps would you take to resolve the problem?

....

Now try to role play this with your group.

Your best friend has found a new friend and you're feeling a little jealous. You feel upset and decide to ignore your friend next time they are around.

How could you fix the situation?

....

What could you do to help your friend to understand your feelings?

....

Now try to role play this with your group.

Glossary

Bee's knees (page 4)
Something that is cool or to think of oneself as cool, special.

Cool as a cucumber (page 15)
Someone who is feeling very calm and in control, even in situations in which they are under pressure.

Confused (page 15)
A person that is unsure and is not thinking clearly.

Cheering up (page 16)
A person who is starting to feel better and is becoming more positive.